WHY IS SHAMBU CHASING THE SMARTPHONE?

Because he is rushing to get on Google Play Store!

That's right!

The Shikari Shambu game is here!

Log on to the Google Play Store NOW!

TINKLE DIGEST

Vol. 27
No. 300

December 2016
100 pages

TINKLE DIGEST

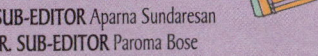

EDITOR Rajani Thindiath
ASSISTANT EDITOR Sean D'mello
SUB-EDITOR Aparna Sundaresan
JR. SUB-EDITOR Paroma Bose
GROUP ART DIRECTOR
Savio Mascarenhas
ARTISTS Archana Amberkar,
Vineet Nair
COLOURING AND LAYOUT Umesh Sarode,
Prasad Sawant
STUDIO COORDINATOR Pranay Bendre
EDITORIAL ASSISTANT Jubel D'Cruz

PRODUCTION
PRODUCTION HEAD Devendra Satpute
PRODUCTION TEAM Dhanad Patil, Shrikant Wagle

CEO Anuraag Agarwal
PRESIDENT Sanjay Dhar
COO M. Krishna Kiran
BUSINESS HEAD (Tinkle) Shriya Ghate
GROUP CREATIVE DIRECTOR Neel Debdutt Paul
SR. MANAGER-Subscription & Customer Service
Surekha Pendse

MANAGER-Legal & Compliance
Anirudh Bhatt

MARKETING MANAGER Achin Jha
BRAND EXECUTIVE Prashob Nair
MARKETING EXECUTIVE Priyanka Gupta

 digest.editor@ack-media.com
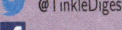 @TinkleDigest
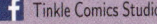 Tinkle Comics Studio

Disclaimer:
In no event will Amar Chitra Katha Pvt. Ltd., be liable for any loss or damage including without limitation, indirect or consequential loss or damage arising from or in connection with the use of Free Gifts/Samples.

ADVERTISING SALES
Sr. Vice President (National)
Eric D'souza +91-9820056421
Assistant Account Director-Print & Online (West)
Rahul Singhania (rahul.singhania@ack-media.com)
Key Account Manager (Mumbai)
Pranuthi Kurma (pranuthi.kurma@ack-media.com)
Deputy General Manager-Print & Online (Delhi)
Raj Mani Patel (rajmani.patel@ack-media.com)
Key Account Manager (Delhi)
Aakansha Deopa (aakansha.deopa@ack-media.com)
Consultant (Delhi)
Jaswinder Gill (jaswinder.gill@ack-media.com)
Sr. Account Director (Bengaluru-South)
S.M. Meenakshi (sm.meenakshi@ack-media.com)
Consultant (Chennai)
Shankar Jayaraman (shankar.j@ack-media.com)
Authorized Representative (Eastern Region)
Jain Enterprises, Kolkata
+91-33-22488257 (bcjain@vsnl.com)
Assistant Manager (Scheduling)
Sandeep Palande (sandeep.palande@ack-media.com)

ADVERTISING ENQUIRIES
advertisingsales@ack-media.com
+91-22-49188811

SALES: sales@ack-media.com

NEWS STAND SALES
Director: Abizar A. Shaikh (abizar@ibhworld.com)
Regional Head: Rajeev Amberkar (rajeev@ibhworld.com)

© **Amar Chitra Katha Pvt. Ltd.,**
Printed & published by Anuraag Agarwal on behalf of Amar Chitra Katha Private Limited, printed at Indigo Press (India) Private Limited, plot no. 1C/716, opp. Dadoji Konddeo Cross Road, between Sussex & Retiwala Industrial Estates, Byculla (E), Mumbai 400027
and published at Amar Chitra Katha Pvt. Ltd., Unit No. 201 & 202, Sumer Plaza, 2nd Floor, Marol Maroshi Road, Andheri (East), Mumbai 400059
Editor: Rajani Thindiath
Subscriptions: tinklesubscription@ack-media.com
For Consumer Complaints, Contact Tel:+91-22-49188881/82/83/84; working hours from 10 am to 6 pm, Mon-Sat
Email: customerservice@ack-media.com

Enquiries: contact@ibhworld.com
IBH Books and Magazines Distributors Pvt. Ltd.
Distribution Offices: North – Delhi
East – Kolkata   **West** – Mumbai
South – Bengaluru, Chennai,
Hyderabad, Thiruvananthapuram

TINKLE CHATTER!

Hooja (excited): Tantri! Did you hear that? We've hit 300!

Suppandi (alarmed): Why are we hitting 300 people, Raja Hooja?

Hooja: Suppandi, I meant *Tinkle Digest* has completed 300 issues!

Suppandi: Whoa! That's a huge number!

Shambu (licking his lips): So when's the party?

Tantri (muttering to himself): And are you cutting the cake, fat brains? Then I'll start hunting for an explosive!

Suppandi: Hohoho!

Tantri (muttering): There he goes again.

Hooja: What is it, Suppandi?

Suppandi: Oh-hoho! Those Defective Detectives! They can never get one thing right!

Tantri (rolling his eyes): Pot. Kettle. Black!

Suppandi: And-and… he-he-he! That story, 'Fresh Fish Sold Here'? People are never satisfied no matter how you follow their instructions! Ask me!

Shambu: Hahaha! Now Nasruddin Hodja's smart at giving and taking instructions. Just check out 'The Thousand Coins'!

Tantri (to reader): These guys can go on like this for another 300 issues and more! We hope you will be along with us on this ride. And hopefully one issue when I finally get rid of that lump of lard! Hmph!

DEFECTIVE DETECTIVES
ALL THAT GLITTERS

Story	Script	Art	Letters
Mirnalini Sarin	Ashwini Falnikar	Abhijeet Kini	Prasad Sawant

THE DEFECTIVE DETECTIVES WERE SPENDING THEIR VACATION WITH RAVI'S UNCLE, VIJAY.

THAT'S A SIX!

EEK! URGH...!

Chipick chipick

HEY! WHAT ARE YOU DOING HERE?

YIKES! ME? I... THE BALL...

SHOO OFF FROM HERE, BOY. IT IS SLIPPERY.

THAT EVENING —

AGENT DUMB CHARADES, I HAVE SOME CLASSIFIED INFORMATION.

YOU DO? WHAT IS IT?

IN THE MORNING, WHEN I WENT TO FETCH THE BALL NEAR THE MARSHLAND, A POLICEMAN WAS INVESTIGATING THE SITE.

WAS HE SECRETIVE ABOUT IT, AGENT RAPIDFIRE?

TOTALLY!

WHAT GOLD CHAIN?

MRS. DUBEY'S GOLD CHAIN WENT MISSING LAST NIGHT. THE POLICE ARE ON THE LOOKOUT FOR THE THIEF.

SO YOU SOLVED THE CASE, I SUPPOSE, WITHOUT KNOWING WHAT IT WAS ABOUT? (SNIGGER, SNIGGER!)

WELL, I AM DETERMINED TO CATCH THE THIEF. GOOD LUCK, BOYS.

THE PICTURE IS CRYSTAL CLEAR, AGENT DUMB CHARADES, ISN'T IT?

UMM... HOW?

THE MAN IS A POLICE OFFICER BY DAY AND A CROOK BY NIGHT. HE PRETENDS TO SOLVE THE CRIMES HE COMMITS.

PANCHNAMA

HORRIBLE! WHAT DO WE DO? HOW DO WE GET HOLD OF HIM?

FEAR NOT, AGENT DUMB CHARADES. WE WILL SET A TRAP AT THE MARSHLAND. THERE'S NO BETTER HIDING PLACE FOR HIM.

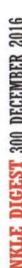

AND ENDED UP CATCHING MY POOR TWIN. HE WORKS NIGHT SHIFTS IN THE DISTRICT CLINIC, YOU KNOW.

THAT EXPLAINS THE INSTRUMENTS HE CARRIES. THEY WERE **MEDICAL** INSTRUMENTS.

HAH HAH HAH HAH... DID YOU THINK I WAS RUNNING AROUND WITH LOCK-PICKING TOOLS?

AND I HAVE SOLVED THE MYSTERY OF THE GOLD CHAIN ROBBERY. HERE IT IS!

HUH?! WHRE IS THE THIEF?

WAAAA!

THERE SHE IS!

THE BABY?! HOW DID YOU KNOW WHERE TO LOOK?

THE BABY IS FASCINATED BY GLITTERY THINGS, YOU KNOW. SHE WAS ABOUT TO DO AWAY WITH MY EARRING ONCE... THAT'S WHAT GAVE ME THE IDEA OF FINDING OUT WHERE SHE STORES ALL HER TREASURE.

SIMPLE LOGIC! BRILLIANT! BOYS, YOU SHOULD LEARN SOMETHING FROM HER.

THIS IS A NEW LOW! BEATEN BY A BABY!

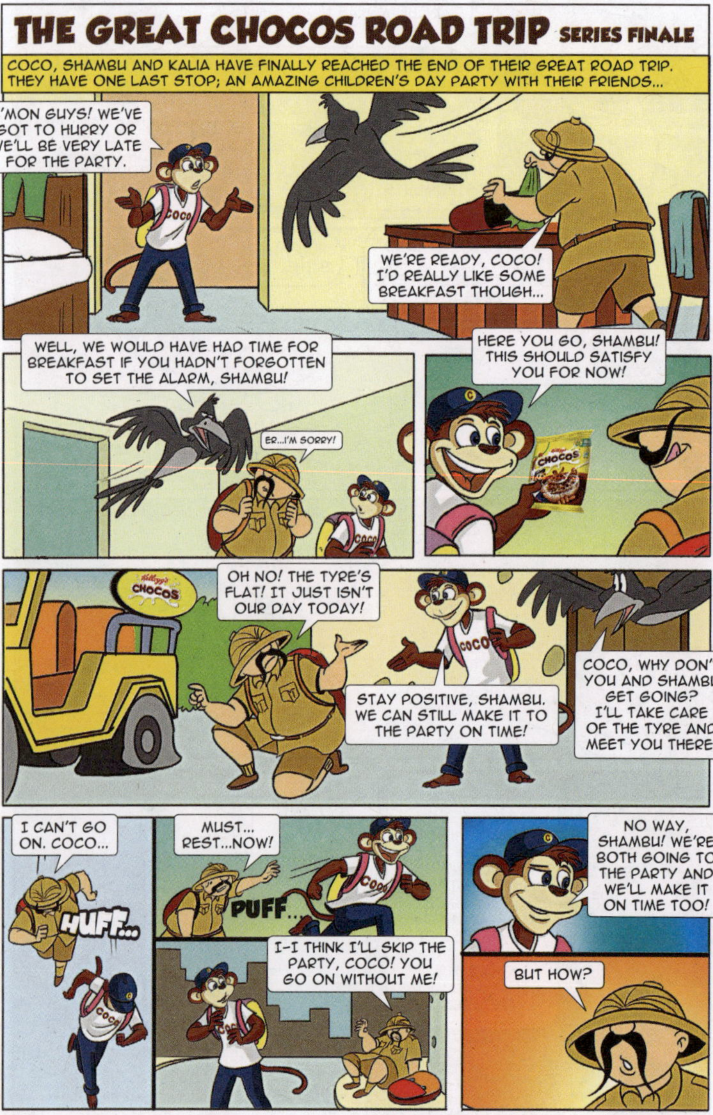

THE GREAT CHOCOS ROAD TRIP SERIES FINALE

COCO, SHAMBU AND KALIA HAVE FINALLY REACHED THE END OF THEIR GREAT ROAD TRIP. THEY HAVE ONE LAST STOP; AN AMAZING CHILDREN'S DAY PARTY WITH THEIR FRIENDS...

C'MON GUYS! WE'VE GOT TO HURRY OR WE'LL BE VERY LATE FOR THE PARTY.

WE'RE READY, COCO! I'D REALLY LIKE SOME BREAKFAST THOUGH...

WELL, WE WOULD HAVE HAD TIME FOR BREAKFAST IF YOU HADN'T FORGOTTEN TO SET THE ALARM, SHAMBU!

ER...I'M SORRY!

HERE YOU GO, SHAMBU! THIS SHOULD SATISFY YOU FOR NOW!

OH NO! THE TYRE'S FLAT! IT JUST ISN'T OUR DAY TODAY!

STAY POSITIVE, SHAMBU. WE CAN STILL MAKE IT TO THE PARTY ON TIME!

COCO, WHY DON'T YOU AND SHAMBU GET GOING? I'LL TAKE CARE OF THE TYRE AND MEET YOU THERE.

I CAN'T GO ON. COCO...

HUFF...

MUST... REST...NOW!

PUFF...

I-I THINK I'LL SKIP THE PARTY, COCO! YOU GO ON WITHOUT ME!

NO WAY, SHAMBU! WE'RE BOTH GOING TO THE PARTY AND WE'LL MAKE IT ON TIME TOO!

BUT HOW?

BY HITCHING A RIDE! IF I'M RIGHT, THOSE ARE OUR ALIEN FRIENDS, HEADING FOR THE PARTY AS WELL. THEY CAN GIVE US A LIFT THERE.

BUT... BUT HOW WILL WE GET THEIR ATTENTION?

WITH THESE!

FUNDOO BALLS? HMMM... A BIG BOWL OF CHOCOS WOULD GET MY ATTENTION!

HA HA HA! THAT'S NOT WHAT I HAD IN MIND, SHAMBU! LET ME SHOW YOU.

THERE! THAT SHOULD GET THEIR ATTENTION!

THANKS FOR STOPPING AND GIVING US A RIDE!

NO PROBLEM, COCO. HAPPY TO BE OF SERVICE.

I CAN'T BELIEVE WE MADE IT, AND THAT TOO RIGHT ON TIME!

YOU SHOULD THANK OUR ALIEN FRIENDS!

IT'S ALSO THANKS TO YOUR FUNDOO BALL IDEA! I DON'T KNOW WHAT WE WOULD DO WITHOUT YOU, COCO!

Kellogg's CHOCOS TINKLE
Children's Day Party

And so, Coco and Shambu joined Suppandi and a bunch of our readers for an amazing Children's Day Bash!

1. Coco, Shambu and Suppandi welcome the the young guests! **2.** The trio join the kids in a game of "Longest Line!" **3.** Ever played "Suppandi Says"? These kids have their feet up because Suppandi said so! **4.** A young guest takes a shot at feeding Shambu Chocos!

5. Shambu and Suppandi are surprised by a birthday cake from Coco! **6.** Our guests pose for a group photo with their amazing gift hampers courtesy Kelloggs and Tinkle! **7.** The kids take a ride in Coco's jeep with Suppandi, Shambu and Coco!

Exciting games, non-stop dancing, hilarious cartoons and amazing gifts!
This Children's Day was definitely something no one would ever forget!

SUPPANDI — A Sticky Situation

Writer Shruti Dave
Illustrator Archana Amberkar
Colourist Umesh Sarode
Letterer Prasad Sawant

WHY CATS AND RATS ARE ENEMIES

Readers' Choice

Illustrations: Vasant Halbe

Based on a story sent by Pradeep Menon, Bombay.

LONG AGO WHEN CATS AND RATS WERE FRIENDS, A CAT AND A RAT FOUND A POT OF TREACLE.

MMM... DELICIOUS!

LET'S FINISH IT!

LET'S NOT BE GREEDY. LET'S KEEP IT FOR THE COMING WINTER.

THAT'S A GOOD IDEA!

THEY FOUND A LONELY SPOT, DUG A HOLE...

...AND HID THE POT IN IT.

THERE! IT'S SAFE NOW!

OUR LITTLE SECRET!

THAT NIGHT THE CAT COULD NOT SLEEP.

I MUST HAVE SOME OF THAT TREACLE...

NEXT MORNING—

I GOT UP LAST NIGHT AND FOUND YOU MISSING.

I HAD GONE TO...

...TO ATTEND MY SISTER'S WEDDING.

REALLY? WHICH SISTER? WHAT'S HER NAME?

HER NAME IS... TOP-GONE.

A WEEK LATER—

I MUST HAVE A LITTLE MORE OF THAT TREACLE.

JUST A LITTLE!

DELICIOUS! ABSOLUTELY DELICIOUS!

OH! I'VE EATEN ALMOST HALF OF IT!

WHEN THE CAT RETURNED HOME—

AH! THERE YOU ARE AT LAST! WHERE WERE YOU?

I HAD TO ATTEND THE WEDDING OF MY SECOND SISTER... HALF-GONE.

AND YET A WEEK LATER, WHEN THE CAT WHO WAS MISSING AGAIN, RETURNED HOME—

DON'T TELL ME YOU WENT TO ATTEND YOUR SISTER'S WEDDING, TODAY, TOO!

I DID! HOW CLEVER OF YOU TO GUESS!

IT WAS THE WEDDING OF MY FAVOURITE SISTER, ALL-GONE!

I WONDER HOW MANY MORE SISTERS HE HAS!

SOON THE WINTER SET IN.

FRIEND, LET'S GO AND DIG OUT OUR PRECIOUS POT TODAY.

UH-UH? ALL RIGHT, LET'S GO.

WHEN THE POT WAS BROUGHT OUT AND OPENED...

HEY! THERE'S NOTHING IN HERE... IT'S ALL GONE.

ALL-GONE!

TOP-GONE! HALF-GONE! YOUR SISTERS INDEED!

ER... FRIEND... LISTEN... AFTER ALL...

YOU... YOU RASCAL! YOU CHEAT! YOU...

STOP IT!

ANOTHER WORD AND YOU'LL BE ALL-GONE TOO!

I'LL TELL THE WHOLE WORLD WHAT A THIEF YOU ARE!

I'LL EAT YOU UP BEFORE YOU DO!

Halbe

HA! HA! TRY AGAIN!

THIEF! THIEF! THIEF!

EVER SINCE CATS AND RATS HAVE BEEN ENEMIES. AND TO THIS DAY RATS SHRIEK "THIEF! THIEF!" WHEN A CAT CHASES THEM.

TINKLE Tricks & Treats

A

What is the major mistake in this picture?

D

Make your own RACING FISH

You will need :
A few colourful plastic tongue-cleaners, a pair of scissors, a few bits of camphor, a bowl of water, a sheet of newspaper.

Cut the tongue-cleaner into fish shapes like this:-

Without touching the water with your fingers, drop each fish carefully into the bowl of water. They should swim about like this:-

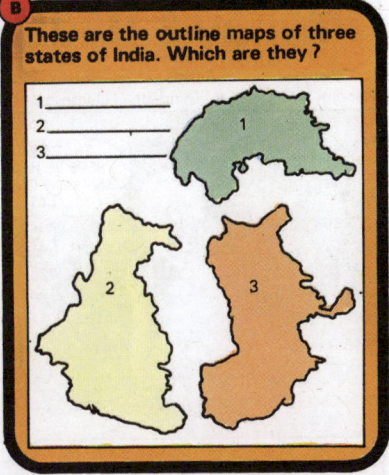

B

These are the outline maps of three states of India. Which are they?

1 _____
2 _____
3 _____

C

Name the missing animal.

?

_ _ _ _ _ _ _ _ _ _

How stick a bit of camphor into each fish like this:-

If they don't, dip a sheet of newspaper, the size of a page from your exercise book, into the water, WITHOUT TOUCHING THE WATER WITH YOUR FINGERTIPS. Now watch them go into action.

Answers:
A—The red signal says 'GO instead of 'STOP'.
B—1. Karnataka 2. Maharashtra 3. Uttar Pradesh
C—Snake.

Pranav's Dadi and the Baby

Story Nandini Nayar **Script** Rajani Thindiath **Illustrations** Durgesh Velhal **Colours** Snehangshu Mazumder **Letters** Pranay Bendre

LATER —

SO, HOW DID IT GO?

WE JOINED SATISH AND THE OTHERS AT THE BABY'S HOUSE.

AND?

IT WAS SO BORING. ALL THE BABY DOES IS GO GA-GA GOO-GOO! HE CAN'T EVEN WALK!

GIVE IT TIME.

A FEW DAYS LATER —

PRANAV'S LOOKING HAPPIER BUT THE BOYS HAVE NOT BEEN BACK ON THE PLAYGROUND...

PRANAV, ARE THINGS WORKING OUT?

NOT YET. YOU KNOW DADI, THE BOYS ACTUALLY FIGHT TO HOLD THE BABY AND THEN THEY CLAP WHEN HE DOES SOMETHING SILLY, LIKE THROW A BALL! SHEESH!

THE DAYS PASSED AND STILL THERE WAS NO SIGN OF THE CHILDREN ON THE PLAYGROUND —

PRANAV, WHERE ARE YOUR FRIENDS? IT'S BEEN QUITE A WHILE NOW, HASN'T IT?

IT'LL TAKE A FEW MORE DAYS, DADI. IT'S NOT SO EASY.

NOT SO EASY? YET WHY ISN'T HE LOOKING MORE UPSET?

SOMETHING'S FISHY.

THE NEXT TIME PRANAV WENT OUT TO MEET HIS FRIENDS —

THIS IS SO SILLY. I HOPE PRANAV DOESN'T CATCH ME FOLLOWING HIM.

HAHAHA... THE BABY'S SO FUNNY!

THAT SHOULD BE THE HOUSE.

AH! NOW I UNDERSTAND THE ATTRACTION.

LATER, WHEN PRANAV CAME BACK HOME —

SO, PRANAV, YOU TOO HAVE GROWN ATTACHED TO THE BABY, HUH?

I CAN'T KEEP AWAY, DADI. THE TOYS ARE SO GOOD!

TOYS?

THE BABY'S TOYS. HE HAS SO MANY OF THEM—CARS, TRUCKS, A TRAIN SET, AEROPLANES, AND HE CAN'T PLAY WITH ANY OF THEM!

SO, ALL YOU SHAMELESS BOYS GO THERE TO PLAY WITH THE BABY'S TOYS?

THE BABY'S CUTE BUT... YEAH.

HAHAHA... HOW SILLY!

WHAT?

...A TRAIN SET WITH TUNNELS AND STATIONS, AND A LAPTOP WITH GAMES AND... DADI, ARE YOU EVEN **LISTENING** TO ME?

YOU! PRETENDING TO FIND THE BABY BORING AND THEN PLAYING... WITH HIS TOYS!

BUT DADI, HE'S GOT AMAZING TOYS! THERE'S A REMOTE OPERATED ROBOT AND A MINI KEYBOARD PLAYER... AND...

BUT DADI WAS TOO BUSY LAUGHING AT SILLY PRANAV AND HIS FRIENDS.

DAFFY DONKEY'S TRICK

Based on a story sent by:
Shashank Bharadwaj, *Karnataka*
Illustrations: Prachi Killekar

THE HARES OF APPU FOREST WERE SAD.

BOO HOO! ALL MY GREENS HAVE GONE AGAIN.

THIS IS GOING TOO FAR. FATTY MUST BE STOPPED.

FATTY THE ELEPHANT WAS ALWAYS TRAMPLING THEIR VEGETABLE PATCHES AND PULLING OUT THE PLANTS JUST FOR FUN.

PIPPY, THE HARE, WENT TO MEET HIS FRIEND, THE WISE DAFFY DONKEY.

DD, WE MUST DO SOMETHING TO STOP FATTY FROM DESTROYING ANY MORE OF OUR VEGETABLE PATCHES.

HMM...HE NEEDS TO STOP THROWING HIS WEIGHT AROUND. I WILL TRY AND SPEAK TO HIM.

NOW LOOK HERE, FATTY, THE HARES ARE VERY UNHAPPY. YOU ARE TRAMPLING ON THEIR GREENS EVERY DAY.

AND I WILL CONTINUE TO DO SO.

BE OFF, YOU!

DON'T, FATTY!

OWW!

HA HA HA!

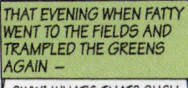

THAT EVENING WHEN FATTY WENT TO THE FIELDS AND TRAMPLED THE GREENS AGAIN —

OWW! WHAT'S THAT? OUCH, SOMETHING'S STINGING MY TRUNK!

HEH HEH HEH! LIKE DESTROYING OUR GREENS NOW, FATTY?

DAFFY POURED SUGARCANE JUICE ON THE PLANTS TO ATTRACT THE ANTS. AND NOW YOU HAVE ANTS INSIDE YOUR TRUNK! SERVES YOU RIGHT.

I'M REALLY SORRY, PIPPY. I'LL NEVER TRAMPLE YOUR GREENS AGAIN.

THE GENEROUS HOST

- A folktale from Tamil Nadu

Script: Luis M. Fernandes
Illustrations: Ram Waeerkar

ONCE UPON A TIME THERE WAS A POOR BUT GENEROUS MAN. ONE DAY—

THERE ARE SOME MEN OUTSIDE. THEY SAY, YOU INVITED THEM TO LUNCH.

AH, YES!

I FORGOT TO TELL YOU ABOUT IT!

WHY ARE YOU ALWAYS INVITING PEOPLE TO LUNCH WHEN WE HAVE NOTHING TO OFFER THEM?

THERE IS NOT A GRAIN OF RICE IN THE HOUSE!

SSSSH! DON'T SHOUT! THEY MIGHT HEAR YOU!

DON'T WORRY ABOUT THE FOOD. I'LL GO OUT AND GET SOMETHING.

WELCOME, MY FRIENDS. WELCOME! PLEASE COME IN.

MAY WE VISIT THE TEMPLE FIRST?

CERTAINLY! FOOD WILL BE READY BY THE TIME YOU RETURN.

FOOD! HAH! HE'LL JUST WANDER AROUND AND COME BACK EMPTY-HANDED.

I'LL HAVE TO GET THOSE MEN TO LEAVE BEFORE HE RETURNS.

SOMETIME LATER WHEN THE GUESTS RETURNED—

COME IN, COME IN!

MY HUSBAND HAS JUST GONE OUT BUT HE'LL BE BACK SOON.

!

WHAT ARE YOU LOOKING AT?

OH! THAT! IT'S MY HUSBAND'S DEITY.

HE WORSHIPS A MORTAR AND PESTLE?!

HE DOES! AND I SHOULDN'T BE TELLING YOU THIS, BUT...

...WHEN HE COMES HOME, HE'LL PICK UP THAT PESTLE AND KNOCK ALL OF YOU ON THE HEADS WITH IT.

LET'S GET OUT OF HERE, BROTHERS.

THAT'S THE ONLY WAY OF PLEASING THIS DEITY.

THIS IS A MADHOUSE!

AS THE GUESTS RUSHED AWAY—

HEY!

WHAT'S THE MATTER? WHY ARE THEY GOING AWAY? AND THAT TOO IN SUCH A HURRY?

THEY ASKED ME FOR THIS PESTLE AND I DID NOT GIVE IT TO THEM.

WHAT!

TINKLE DIGEST 300 DECEMBER 2016

HEADLINES FROM YESTERYEARS

TINKLE TIMES

From India, With Love (India)

The world's largest letter of love and friendship, signed by thousands of Indian children, was handed over recently to 15,000 children in Lahore, Pakistan. The letter says, 'Dear children of Pakistan, let's join our hearts in friendship. Together, we can make a better world - from the children of India'. The 7,780-square-metre letter is made of tarpaulin and is written in Hindi, Urdu and English. The brainchild of the non-governmental organization 'Friends Without Borders', the letter was first exhibited in Bengaluru and then later in Mumbai, before being sent to Pakistan.

No Joke (Germany)

A German man has been ordered to stop laughing out loud in the woods after joggers complained he was disturbing the peace. Joachim Bahrenfeld from Datteln said he goes to the woods after work and at weekends

to have a good laugh. But Bahrenfeld now faces a £4,000 fine or six months in jail if he laughs out loud again, after a jogger took him to court saying he was disturbing the peace. German laugh expert Susanne Maier, who founded the German Laughter Academy, took Bahrenfeld's side. She said he was just having a good old giggle. Maier added that the person who made the complaint should learn the benefits of laughing.

Grand Old Tortoise (India)

Adwaita, the 255-year-old giant tortoise that used to attract crowds at Alipore Zoo in Kolkata, passed away in March 2006.

British seamen brought the 250-kg male tortoise from the Seychelles Islands to Kolkata more than two centuries ago. According to zoo officials, Adwaita was a gift for Robert Clive of the East India Company and it spent several years in his gardens. The tortoise was shifted to Alipore Zoo about 130 years ago.

"It's a mercy the rain has finally stopped," sighed Inspector Jai wearily as he rolled down the window of his car.

"I agree," joined in Detective Veeru, leaning back in his seat. "First, we drive for miles in response to what turns out to be a prank call, then we're greeted by torrential, unseasonal rain and now… looks like we're out of fuel."

Glancing at the fuel gauge to confirm this, Inspector Jai grimaced, "Let's hope we find a petrol pump before the car gives up on us."

A petrol pump came along soon enough and as they pulled into it, they spotted a police car and an ambulance leaving.

"What happened here?" Inspector Jai addressed one of the constables on the scene, flashing his ID.

"Robbery, Sir," replied the constable, saluting smartly. "The attendant was shot at. A witness saw two men get into a van and drive off. We found the van abandoned outside a campers' park, a few kilometres from here. Sub-inspector Patel is there now, rounding up suspects."

"I vote we head to this park. Might as well do something productive on this waste of a day," said Detective Veeru.

Inspector Jai agreed and after refilling the car's fuel tank, they drove towards the park, accompanied by the constable. Outside the park, they found the sub-inspector about to drive off. They stopped him, introduced themselves and asked if they could help. The sub-inspector told them that he had identified three pairs of suspects in the park, but could not arrest anyone due to lack of evidence. The duo decided to interrogate the suspects themselves.

The first pair had built a fire outside their tent and were frying fish over it. "My friend and I are on a hiking trip. We came here last night and went fishing, a little before the rain began this afternoon. Some catch we've got. Would you like some?" said Raj Rane, one of them, offering some freshly fried fish. The duo declined politely and moved on to the next pair of suspects who were inside their tent pitched atop a small hill in the park. One of them, Satya Johar, said, "We set up the tent this morning and went out to buy some provisions. We've been indoors ever since." He picked up his rucksack from the wet grass and kept it on the cot as Inspector Jai and Detective Veeru vacated it to leave.

The third and final pair of suspects was in a van. John D'Costa, its owner, was curt. "We haven't left the van all day because of the darn rain. Are you going to arrest people for playing cards now?"

"Well, that's that," said Inspector Jai, once they had stepped out of the van and away from John D'Costa's surly presence. "What say we make some arrests now?"

"Suits me just fine," grinned Detective Veeru. "Time to make some 'provisions' for Satya Johar and his partner."

How did the duo deduce that the second pair of suspects was guilty?

Answer to You Be the Detective: Satya Johar said that he and his friend had set up their tent that morning, before the rain began. The tent was pitched atop a small hill which meant that water could not flow into it from any slope or depression. Yet, the grass inside the tent was wet. Thus, Satya was lying and the tent had been set up after the rain had begun.

Kalia
THE CROW

Script:
LUIS

Illustrations:
PRADEEP SATHE

ONE DAY AS KALIA WAS FLYING PAST THE RIVER —

THERE'S DOOB-DOOB AND CHAMATAKA.

DOOB-DOOB LOOKS VERY HAPPY. I WONDER WHAT THEY ARE TALKING ABOUT.

BE CAREFUL, CHAMATAKA. KALIA HAS SETTLED ON A TREE BEHIND US.

HE COULD SPOIL ALL OUR PLANS. I'LL TAKE HIM AWAY FROM HERE.

OH, KALIA, I WAS LOOKING FOR YOU.

YOU WERE?

SOMEBODY HAS LEFT A LOT OF RICE ON THE SHORE FURTHER DOWN. LOVELY, FLUFFY RICE. I'LL TAKE YOU THERE. COME ON!

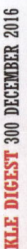

COME ON, KALIA.

THEY DON'T WANT ME HERE. I WONDER WHY?

THEY'LL BE BACK SOON... IF ONLY I KNEW WHO THEY WERE WAITING FOR...

...SHONAR! WERE THEY WAITING FOR HIM? I WONDER WHY HE LOOKS SO WORRIED.

WHAT'S THE MATTER, SHONAR?

NOTHING, KALIA. I AM JUST LOOKING AT MY REFLECTION IN THE WATER.

ARE THERE ANY LEAVES GROWING ON MY ANTLERS?

LEAVES? OF COURSE NOT. WHO TOLD YOU THERE WERE LEAVES GROWING ON YOUR ANTLERS?

CHAMATAKA.

AND I SUPPOSE HE TOLD YOU TO COME HERE AND LOOK AT YOUR REFLECTION TOO.

HE DID.

HEY, KALIA, I HOPE THERE'S NO DANGER HERE.

THERE WAS, BUT IT HAS GONE TO THE OTHER SIDE.

TAIL TALK
WITH MANEKA GANDHI

We share our planet with almost 30 million other species of life forms. And there is so much that we need to know about them.

Mrs. **Maneka Gandhi** is a renowned activist-politician who has worked tirelessly for animal welfare and the environment. She has authored several books and articles on the subjects.

Is there any law/act that protects monkeys from *madaris** and ensures their welfare?

No person in India is allowed to capture, own, buy, sell or train any wild animal for public exhibition. The animals used by *madaris*, i.e. monkeys, snakes, bears, mongooses and parakeets, are all protected by the Wildlife Protection Act, 1972. Section 22 of the Prevention of Cruelty to Animals Act, 1960, is also applicable. Under both these Acts, the *madaris* can be arrested on the spot, and the animal confiscated and handed over to the Wildlife Department, a zoo or a local animal welfare shelter. In case of healthy snakes, mongooses or birds, the animals could be released into a jungle.

Art: Prabha Mallya

How are geese as pets?
Both ducks and geese can make wonderful pets. It is easy to bond with them. I have 150 in my animal shelter and they are friendly and sociable. If anyone wants to adopt them, they are welcome – provided they have a pond in their house.

My Labrador jumps on me and licks me a lot. What should I do to stop this habit?
– Rishik Sood, Delhi

This is not just affection but power play. The jumping needs to be stopped. The best way to do so is to turn your back on your Labrador as soon as it starts jumping, and walk away. You can also bend your knee and hold it in front to block its jump. Accompany this with a firm, verbal 'No'. It may take a little time but your dog will get the message.

* Animal tamers who use them for making money

My dog has a habit of going outside, but it does not return for a long time. Why?
– *Payal Shetty, Udupi, Karnataka*

This behaviour probably means that your dog is going to find food elsewhere; it may be a garbage dump or someone else's house. For the sake of your dog's health, I suggest you increase its mealtimes to four instead of one or two. Feed it at 8 a.m., 1 p.m., 4 p.m. and 8 p.m. The meals can be smaller in size. Let it out after each meal but stand outside and call for it after five minutes.

It is also possible that it is going out to find a mate. I suggest you have it sterilized immediately.

Is it healthy to feed my pet cat packaged food every day? What should a pet cat's daily diet consist of?

A cat's diet should consist of 60% protein, usually in some form of meat and soya; eggs are allowed once a week. Lightly steam or boil the meat and use the broth from the meat to flavour the rice and vegetables. This way, you can cut down on the meat and add more soya.

Approximately 20% of the diet should be composed of vegetables like lightly-steamed carrots, cauliflowers, or any other vegetable that your cat enjoys. Try different ones.

The grain content of the diet should be about 20% including rice, amaranth, oatmeal, barley and millet. The grains should be well-cooked and can be mixed and served with brown rice.

A vitamin and mineral supplement is also essential for a complete diet. It is important to ensure that cats get enough of the essential amino acid, taurine, a deficiency of which can lead to blindness. A minimum of twice a day and ideally thrice, is recommended.

If it is not possible to cook for your pet, then try and find a natural pet food with no artificial colouring or flavourings. Especially avoid preservatives such as BHA, BHT or ethoxyquin, which may increase chances of liver cancer. Try and mix in some extra vegetables or grains each day, followed by the vitamin and mineral supplement.

Cats on a non-packaged diet will probably eat and drink less and pass less stool, since the food they are eating is nutritionally more complete with much fewer fillers and waste products.

If you have been feeding it packaged food and want to change over, introduce the new diet gradually over a few days, mixing it in with the usual one, as too sudden a change in diet can lead to vomiting and diarrhoea. After about a week, when your pet is eating the diet well, then phase out the pet food entirely.

The chief and the glutton

—A Nepalese folktale

Illustrations: V.B. Halbe

Based on a story sent by
**Suraj Ghising Lama
Jalpaiguri**

THE CHIEF OF A VILLAGE BECAME FRIENDLY WITH ONE OF THE VILLAGERS. BUT AFTER SOME TIME HE FOUND THAT THE MAN WAS A GLUTTON.

HOW MUCH HE EATS! AND HE COMES EVERY DAY.

WE MUST STOP HIM FROM COMING SO OFTEN.

THE NEXT EVENING—

HE'LL BE HERE ANY MOMENT NOW. I'M GOING OUT.

TELL HIM WE HAVE ALREADY EATEN AND SEND HIM AWAY AS POLITELY AS YOU CAN.

THE FRIEND CAME AS USUAL

HOW HUNGRY I AM!

I AM SORRY, I HAVE NOTHING TO OFFER YOU.

WE'VE ALREADY EATEN AND THE CHIEF HAS GONE OUT.

OH!

IF HE WERE HERE HE WOULD CERTAINLY HAVE KILLED A CHICKEN FOR YOU.

A CHICKEN!

I LOVE CHICKEN!

WHAT DOES IT MATTER IF THE CHIEF IS NOT AT HOME? I'LL CATCH A CHICKEN...

...AND YOU CAN COOK IT FOR ME,

NO, NO!

WHY NOT?

EH? WELL, I....ER...

...I CAN'T PUT A GUEST TO SUCH TROUBLE. MY HUSBAND WOULD GET TERRIBLY ANGRY.

NONSENSE! IT'S NO TROUBLE AT ALL!

I CAN'T WAIT TO EAT IT.

I'LL TELL HER TO HURRY UP.

WHAT HAPPENED?

EVERYTHING WENT WRONG.

HE INSISTED THAT I COOK A CHICKEN FOR HIM.

ALL RIGHT. NOW LISTEN...

...WHEN THE CHICKEN IS READY GIVE HIM ONLY TWO PIECES.

BUT SERVE THEM IN THE COPPER PLATE WHICH WE KEEP FOR GUESTS.

AND THE REST OF THE CHICKEN?

SERVE IT TO ME— IN AN ORDINARY CLAY POT.

WHEN THE CHICKEN WAS READY, THE WIFE DID AS HER HUSBAND HAD TOLD HER.

WELL, ALL RIGHT. I'LL EAT OUT OF THE COPPER PLATE.

BUT I HOPE WE ARE NOT TROUBLED BY THE EVIL SPIRIT TODAY.

EVIL SPIRIT?

AN EVIL SPIRIT SOMETIMES COMES TO OUR HOUSE AND PUTS OUT THE LIGHT.

IS THAT SO?

I THINK I KNOW WHAT MY HUSBAND HAS IN MIND.

HEY!

WHOOSH!

IN THE DARKNESS, THE CHIEF TRIED TO EXCHANGE THE DISHES...

...BUT BEFORE HE COULD DO SO—

WHAM!

THE EVIL SPIRIT WAS TRYING TO STEAL MY CHICKEN, BUT I WAS TOO QUICK FOR HIM.

NOW IF YOU DON'T MIND I'LL FINISH MY DINNER ELSEWHERE.

OOOOH!

GET UP... ARE YOU ALL RIGHT?

HE HAS GONE AWAY... WITH THE CHICKEN.

THE RASCAL... OUCH!

NEVER MIND! WE'LL FIND A WAY TO OUTWIT HIM TOMORROW.

SUPPANDI Road Rules

Story & Script
Shruti Dave

Pencils & Inks
Archana Amberkar

Colours
Umesh Sarode

Letters
Prasad Sawant

ANU CLUB
IT'S HOTTING UP

By: Margie Sastry

Illustrations: Shyam Desai

CHITRA ARRIVED AT THE USUAL SATURDAY MEETING LOOKING VERY FLUSTERED.

WHAT'S UP, CHITRA? YOU LOOK AS IF YOU'VE SEEN A GHOST!

HAH! HOW CAN MISS SCIENTIFIC SEE ANYTHING SO UNSCIENTIFIC AS A GHOST?

DEEPA WAS MORE SYMPATHETIC THAN THE BOYS.

HUSH, GUYS! DON'T TEASE HER. WHAT'S IT, CHITRA?

I HAD A TERRIBLE NIGHTMARE! I DREAMT THAT THE OZONE LAYER HAD BURST OPEN AND WE WERE ALL ZAPPED BY ULTRAVIOLET RAYS.

HOW LUCKY! YOU GET TO SEE MOVIES FOR FREE IN YOUR DREAMS.

UNCLE ANU, DREAMS AND NIGHTMARES ARE ALL RUBBISH, AREN'T THEY?

WHETHER DREAMS ARE TRUE OR NOT, CHITRA'S DREAM IS A WAKE UP CALL.

BUT THAT'S IMPOSSIBLE. WE CAN'T BE ZAPPED BY UV RAYS FROM SPACE, CAN WE, UNCLE ANU?

WE HAVE HAD SO MANY WARNINGS TO ALERT US THAT WE CANNOT AFFORD TO IGNORE NATURE.

THAT'S TRUE. TSUNAMI AND TIDAL WAVES AND TYPHOONS WERE THINGS WE JUST READ ABOUT IN GEOGRAPHY.

NOW WE KNOW WHAT TREMENDOUS FORCES THEY ARE. THE BEST TECHNOLOGY AND MAN-MADE STRUCTURES CAN BE DESTROYED BY THEM.

ALL COUNTRIES, BIG OR SMALL, DEVELOPED OR DEVELOPING, ARE HELPLESS AGAINST NATURE.

HOW FUNNY! I THOUGHT WE WERE LIVING IN THE MOST SCIENTIFIC AND MODERN AGE, WHERE MAN WAS IN CONTROL AND ON TOP OF THE WORLD.

WELL, IT'S TRUE THAT WE HAVE TECHNOLOGICALLY ADVANCED BUT WE HAVE IGNORED THE IMPACT THAT OUR LIFESTYLE WILL HAVE ON THE ENVIRONMENT.

NOW NATURE IS HITTING BACK HARD. THE EARTH IS HOTTING UP, CARBON DIOXIDE LEVELS ARE RISING, THE OCEAN CURRENTS ARE BECOMING UNPREDICTABLE AND EARTHQUAKES ARE OCCURRING WITH GREATER FREQUENCY.

YOU KNOW, THIS SOUNDS LIKE A KID WHO'S BEEN TAKING A LOT OF FLAK FROM A BULLY AND ONE DAY SUDDENLY DECIDES TO HIT BACK HARD!

YOU PUT IT IN SUCH A SIMPLE WAY, BHARAT.

YES, BUT IT'S SO TRUE. THIS IS THE IDEA THAT LEADERS OF ALL COUNTRIES HAVE BEEN TRYING TO EXPLAIN TO EACH OTHER AT HUGE CONFERENCES - THAT WE MUST DO SOMETHING OR EVERYBODY WILL SUFFER.

IT'S LIKE RING-A-RING OF ROSES. WE ALL FALL DOWN TOGETHER!

YOU ARE RIGHT.

SCIENTISTS SAY THAT THE ENTIRE WESTERN SIBERIAN SUB-ARCTIC REGION HAS BEGUN TO MELT, AND THIS HAS ALL HAPPENED IN THE LAST THREE OR FOUR YEARS. THE GREAT LAKES OF THE U.S., THE PLANET'S LARGEST CONCENTRATION OF FRESH WATER, IS THAWING EARLIER EACH SPRING ACCORDING TO AN ANALYSIS OF ICE BREAK-UPS DATING BACK TO 1846. THESE ARE SERIOUS WARNINGS.

BUT UNCLE ANU, THESE ARE SUCH BIG THINGS AND WE ARE SO SMALL. WHAT CAN WE DO?

OKAY, THEN LET'S THINK OF KID-SIZE SOLUTIONS TO THE GREAT ECOLOGICAL PROBLEMS. WHAT CAN YOU DO, BHARAT? GIVE ME A SOLUTION STARTING WITH B!

BHARAT THOUGHT FOR A WHILE.

BICYCLE RACE! I'LL ORGANISE A RACE TO TELL KIDS ABOUT USING ECO FRIENDLY TRANSPORT LIKE CYCLING, WALKING, AND ROLLER SKATING.

THAT'S A GREAT IDEA! WHO'S NEXT?

C, C, WHAT'S WITH C, LET ME SEE... I'LL ORGANISE A CLEAN-UP CAMPAIGN AROUND OUR COLONY EVERY SUNDAY. WE'LL GATHER ALL THE KIDS OF THE BLOCK TO MAKE SURE THAT NO RUBBISH IS AROUND TO BLOCK DRAINS.

THAT'S A HERCULEAN TASK BUT I'M SURE YOU WILL MANAGE.

I AM NEXT! A IS FOR ART. I'LL HAVE AN ART AND CRAFT CONTEST, USING ONLY RECYCLED MATERIAL.

YES, THERE ARE LOTS OF POSSIBILITIES THERE. THE BACK SIDE OF WALL CALENDARS GIVE YOU GREAT PAPER FOR DRAWING AND YOU CAN MAKE A ZILLION THINGS WITH OLD NEWSPAPER AND NATURAL DYES FROM VEGETABLES. YOU CAN ALSO USE RICE STARCH FOR GLUE.

SEE, WE ALREADY HAVE AN ABC OF KID-SIZE ACTIVITIES! ANY MORE VOLUNTEERS?

OH, UNCLE ANU, YOU SAVED ME. I COULDN'T THINK OF ANYTHING STARTING WITH V. NOW I KNOW - I WILL BECOME A VOLUNTEER FOR OUR LOCAL GROUP THAT WORKS FOR SAVING THE MANGROVES.

THAT LEAVES JUST THE TWO OF US, ANAND. SHOULD WE TEAM UP AND THINK OF SOMETHING?

A AND D? HMMMM. AH, YES. ACTING AND DRAMA. LET'S WRITE A FUNNY SKIT THAT WE CAN PUT UP IN SCHOOL AND IN THE COLONY.

GREAT! I LOVE ANY REASON TO DRESS UP. WOW, WE ARE GOING TO HAVE FUN. I LIKE THAT!

NOW LET'S GO OUT FOR A LONG WALK.

NO, I WANT TO SIT COZILY ON THE COUCH AND WATCH T.V.

OH! THAT REMINDS ME. I MUST TELL YOU ABOUT A SMART INVENTION SOMEONE'S MADE TO CONTROL THE T.V. AND EXERCISE OF TEENAGERS.

HERE IT IS. IN THIS MAGAZINE CALLED NEW SCIENTISTS, THE SHOES – DUBBED SQUARE EYES – CONTAIN AN ELECTRONIC PRESSURE SENSOR AND A TINY COMPUTER CHIP TO RECORD HOW MANY STEPS THE WEARER HAS TAKEN IN A DAY. A WIRELESS TRANSMITTER PASSES THE INFORMATION TO A RECEIVER CONNECTED TO A TELEVISION, AND THIS DECIDES HOW MUCH EVENING VIEWING TIME THE WEARER DESERVES, BASED ON THE DAY'S EXERTIONS.

WOW, THAT'S AWESOME CONTROL! HOW CAN YOU BEAT THAT?

New Scientists

SIMPLE, I WOULD STAND IN FRONT OF THE TV AND DO ON THE SPOT JOGGING!

I WOULD JOG WITH A BOWL OF POPCORN IN ONE HAND AND A COLD DRINK IN THE OTHER.

UNCLE ANU HERDED THEM ALL OUT OF THE HOUSE.

THAT'S WHY I DON'T PLAN TO USE ANY GIZMOS ON YOU CUNNING KIDS! NOW GIDDY UP AND GO RUNNING TO GET RID OF ALL THE CALORIES YOU JUST GUZZLED!

HA HA! YOU MUST HAVE BEEN A CATTLE RANCHER IN YOUR LAST LIFE, UNCLE ANU!

FROM CLAY TABLETS TO *Paper*

Script : Luis M. Fernandes
Illustrations : Pradeep Sathe

THE ANCIENT SUMERIANS USED TO WRITE ON TABLETS OF WET CLAY WITH A TOOL KNOWN AS THE STYLUS.

LATER, THE CLAY TABLETS WERE BAKED IN THE SUN OR IN A POTTER'S OVEN SO THAT THEY WOULD BECOME HARD.

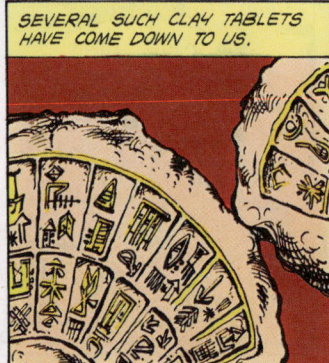

SEVERAL SUCH CLAY TABLETS HAVE COME DOWN TO US.

IT WAS THE EGYPTIANS WHO GAVE PAPYRUS TO THE WORLD.

PAPYRUS WAS MADE FROM THE STALK OF THE PAPYRUS PLANT, A TALL REED WHICH OFTEN GREW TO A HEIGHT OF TWELVE FEET.

THE STALKS WERE CUT INTO THIN STRIPS AND GLUED TOGETHER WITH A PASTE MADE OF FLOUR.

THIS WAS THEN HAMMERED INTO A THIN SHEET AND DRIED IN THE SUN. SEVERAL SUCH SHEETS WERE THEN GLUED TOGETHER TO FORM LONG ROLLS. SOME OF THESE ROLLS WERE OVER A HUNDRED FEET LONG!

PAPYRUS HAD ITS FLAWS. IT SMUDGED EASILY. YET IT BECAME THE CHIEF WRITING MATERIAL OF MUCH OF THE ANCIENT WORLD AND REMAINED SO FOR ALMOST FOUR THOUSAND YEARS.

THE GREEKS AND THE ROMANS TOO USED PAPYRUS.

BUT FOR DAY-TO-DAY WRITING, THE ROMANS USED A WOODEN SLATE COATED WITH BLACK WAX.

WHEN ONE SCRATCHED THROUGH THE WAX, THE LETTERS WOULD STAND OUT.

TO RUB OFF WHAT HAD BEEN WRITTEN, ONE HAD TO HEAT THE SLATE.

THIS WOULD SMOOTHEN THE SURFACE AND THE SLATE OF WAX WOULD BE READY FOR USE AGAIN.

IN INDIA MOST WRITING WAS DONE ON PALM LEAVES...

...BUT LATER, TAMRA PATRAS OR COPPER PLATES WERE USED FOR OFFICIAL RECORDS.

THE CHINESE WERE THE FIRST TO DISCOVER THE ART OF MAKING PAPER.

THEY MADE IT FROM MULBERRY BARK OR RAGS BUT THEY KEPT THE METHOD A CLOSELY-GUARDED SECRET FOR NEARLY SEVEN HUNDRED YEARS.

THEN THE ARABS WHO HAD CONQUERED A CHINESE CITY, PERSUADED SOME OF THEIR PRISONERS TO PART WITH THE SECRET.

AND EUROPEANS IN THEIR TURN LEARNT THE METHOD FROM THE ARABS.

TODAY THE BEST PAPER IS STILL MADE OUT OF RAGS. BUT MOST PAPER IS MADE FROM SPRUCE OR PINE WOOD.

PINE

SPRUCE

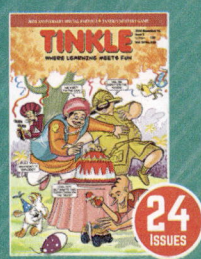
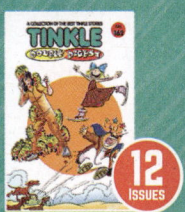

THE THOUSAND COINS
— A Nasruddin Hodja tale

Script: Luis M. Fernandes Illustrations: Ram Waeerkar

NASRUDDIN HODJA HAD A HABIT OF PRAYING ALOUD. AND EVERY DAY HE USED TO PRAY FOR THE SAME THING—AND IN THE SAME WAY.

OH, GOD, GIVE ME ONE THOUSAND GOLD COINS.

ONE THOUSAND COINS, MIND YOU! IF YOU GIVE ME EVEN ONE COIN LESS I WON'T ACCEPT THE MONEY.

ONE DAY HIS NEIGHBOUR DECIDED TO PLAY A TRICK ON HIM. HE PUT NINE HUNDRED AND NINETY-NINE COINS IN A BAG···

···AND THREW IT INTO THE HODJA'S HOUSE.

THUD

A BAG OF COINS! GOD HAS ANSWERED MY PRAYERS!

WHEN THE HODJA COUNTED THE MONEY—

NINE-HUNDRED AND NINETY-NINE COINS!

NOW LET'S SEE WHAT HE DOES.

HE WILL HAVE TO REFUSE THE MONEY BECAUSE IT IS ONE COIN SHORT OF A THOUSAND.

BUT TO HIS NEIGHBOUR'S SURPRISE—

THANK YOU FOR THIS MONEY, GOD!

BUT PLEASE SEE THAT YOU SEND THE REMAINING COIN AS SOON AS YOU CAN.

WHAT A RASCAL YOU ARE, NASRUDDIN! EVEN YOUR PRAYERS ARE FALSE!

ANYWAY, GIVE ME MY MONEY BACK!

YOUR MONEY?

THIS MONEY WAS SENT TO ME BY GOD.

IT WAS I WHO THREW IT INTO YOUR HOUSE.

GOD CHOSE YOU TO DO HIS WORK. NOW PLEASE GO.

NOT WITHOUT MY MONEY!

IT'S NOT YOUR MONEY, I TELL YOU!

LET'S GO TO THE JUDGE.

I AM NOT FEELING TOO WELL. I CAN'T WALK ALL THE WAY TO THE JUDGE.

YOU CAN HAVE MY MULE TO RIDE ON!

BUT I CAN'T APPEAR BEFORE THE JUDGE DRESSED IN THESE OLD ROBES!

AND I HAVE NOTHING ELSE TO WEAR!

DON'T WORRY ABOUT CLOTHES! I'LL LEND YOU MY NEW COAT!

OH, I NEVER REALISED THIS FELLOW WAS SO TRICKY.

SOON —

YOUR HONOUR, LISTEN TO MY STORY! THIS MAN PRAYS LOUDLY EVERY MORNING...

THE NEIGHBOUR SPOKE FOR A LONG TIME. WHEN HE HAD FINISHED—

SO THE BAG OF MONEY WHICH THE HODJA FOUND IS YOURS!

THAT IS THE TRUTH, YOUR HONOUR.

DON'T BELIEVE HIM, YOUR HONOUR. HE IS ALWAYS CLAIMING OTHER PEOPLE'S PROPERTY AS HIS OWN.

I WON'T BE SURPRISED IF HE SAYS THAT THE MULE ON WHICH I RODE HERE IS HIS.

IT IS MINE!

NEXT, YOU'LL SAY THAT THIS COAT TOO IS YOURS!

IT IS! AND WELL YOU KNOW IT.

DO YOU SEE HOW IT IS, YOUR HONOUR?

I DO, INDEED!

IT IS CLEAR TO ME THAT THE BAG OF MONEY TOO IS NOT YOURS!

NOT MINE!

BUT...BUT...

THE CASE IS DISMISSED!

THIS IS MADDENING!

PLEASE HAVE MERCY ON ME, NASRUDDIN. I AM NOT A RICH MAN...

YOU SHOULD HAVE THOUGHT OF THAT EARLIER.

ANYWAY, HERE IS YOUR MONEY.

AND YOUR FUR COAT AND YOUR MULE.

HIS NEIGHBOUR NEVER DARED TO INTERFERE WITH HIM AGAIN.

OH, GOD, SEND ME A THOUSAND COINS...

MEET THE
ELEPHANT

Based on the material provided by
Nandini Deshmukh

Script : Ashvin
Illustrations : Pradeep Sathe

HOW MUCH DOES THIS LARGEST OF LAND ANIMALS WEIGH? ABOUT THREE TO FOUR TONS. WHY, THAT'S OVER 3000 TO 4000 KILOS! YES, AND HOW TALL DO YOU THINK HE IS? ABOUT EIGHT TO TEN FEET? THAT'S RIGHT! HE EATS OVER 200 KILOS OF GRASS, LEAVES, FLOWERS, FRUITS, TWIGS AND BAMBOO SHOOTS EVERY DAY, AND DRINKS ABOUT 200 LITRES OF WATER.

SEE HOW HE SUCKS IN THE WATER WITH HIS TRUNK AND SQUIRTS IT INTO HIS MOUTH.

FOR ALL HIS WEIGHT OUR FRIEND IS VERY LIGHT ON HIS FEET. EVEN WHEN HE TREADS ON DRY LEAVES YOU WOULDN'T HEAR A SOUND! AND HE CAN STRIDE ACROSS A DITCH 8' WIDE WITH EASE.

HERE HE IS— NOW REACHING FOR SOME FRUIT UP ABOVE...

...NOW UPROOTING THE GRASS DOWN BELOW.

SEE HOW HE CLEANS THE MUD OFF THE ROOTS BY FLICKING THE BUNCH AGAINST HIS BENT KNEE.

ONLY THEN DOES HE PUT THE GRASS INTO HIS MOUTH! RATHER A CLEAN FELLOW, ISN'T HE?

BUT YOU WOULDN'T THINK SO IF YOU SAW HIM WALLOWING IN THIS DIRTY, MUDDY POND. HE IS ALONE HERE BUT HE USUALLY MOVES WITH THE HERD. HE FEELS SAFE WITH THE HERD AND THE OLD COW ELEPHANT WHO LEADS THEM.

WHEN HE WAS BORN, TWO COW ELEPHANTS HELPED HIS MOTHER AND TOOK CARE OF BOTH OF THEM.

THEN HIS MOTHER TOOK CARE OF HIM TILL HE WAS ALMOST THREE YEARS OLD. SHE NURSED HIM AND FED HIM AND PROTECTED HIM.

EVEN AFTER THAT, THE ELDERS ALWAYS TOOK CARE OF HIM AS HE WANDERED WITH THE HERD.

YES, IT'S NOT ONLY SAFE TO BE WITH THE HERD BUT IT'S GOOD FUN TOO!

HE HAS COME OUT OF THE WATER, AT LAST. WHY IS HE POUNDING THE SOFT EARTH ON THE BANK?

LOOK! HE'S SPRAYING HIMSELF WITH THE DUST.

PERHAPS HE DOES IT TO PROTECT HIS SKIN FROM THE HEAT OF THE SUN OR FROM THE BLOOD-SUCKING INSECTS THAT TORMENT EVEN ELEPHANTS!

HIS TRUNK IS A WONDERFUL THING, ISN'T IT? IT HELPS HIM TO EAT, TO DRINK, TO SMELL, TO BATHE AND TO SPRAY HIMSELF. WOULD YOU BELIEVE THAT IT'S MADE UP OF 40,000 MUSCLES AND THAT IT CAN PICK UP EVEN A BLADE OF GRASS?

NO WONDER HE TAKES SUCH CARE OF IT. WHEN ATTACKING OR DEFENDING HIMSELF, HE COILS UP HIS TRUNK AND USES ONLY HIS TUSKS. THESE ARE ACTUALLY TWO OF HIS FRONT TEETH WHICH GROW VERY LONG.

HIS ONLY REAL ENEMY IS THE TIGER. BUT EVEN TIGERS SELDOM ATTACK THE ELEPHANT. IT'S TOO RISKY!

THE INDIAN ELEPHANT WHOM YOU HAVE JUST MET IS MUCH SMALLER THAN HIS COUSIN THE AFRICAN ELEPHANT. BUT BOTH OF THEM HAVE A LONG LIFE— BETWEEN SIXTY-FIVE AND A HUNDRED YEARS! DID YOU NOTICE THAT INDIAN COW ELEPHANTS HAVE NO TUSKS?

SMALL EARS

BIG BROAD EARS

SHORTER TUSKS

INDIAN ELEPHANT

LONGER TUSKS

AFRICAN ELEPHANT

ONE LIP

FIVE TOES

FOUR TOES

TWO LIPS

FOUR TOES

THREE TOES

TINKLE DIGEST 300 DECEMBER 2016

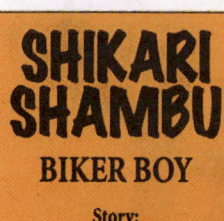

SHIKARI SHAMBU

BIKER BOY

Story:
L.R. Raja Baskar

Script:
Janaki Viswanathan

Illustrations:
Savio Mascarenhas

ONE AFTERNOON —

SHANTI, WHAT DO YOU THINK OF MY NEW MODE OF TRANSPORT?

A MOTORBIKE!!

VRRROOM

I'VE DECIDED TO CALL HER TUR-TUR. AND DON'T MISS MY HELMET.

BIKER BOY? OOH! LET'S GO ON A BIKE RIDE RIGHT NOW.

LET'S GO TO THE FUN FAIR NEAR THE MARKET.

TO THE FUN FAIR THEN, TUR-TUR.

WHAT SORT OF BIKER BOY ARE YOU, SHAMBU? YOU'RE SUPPOSED TO SPEED ALONG.

NO, NO. DRIVE SAFE, THAT'S MY MOTTO. RIGHT, TUR-TUR?

AT THE FAIR—

MELA

I'LL JUST PARK HER AND JOIN YOU.

ALL RIGHT.

SHAMBU SPENT QUITE SOME TIME PARKING HIS TUR-TUR.

HOTEL.

BIKER BOY

HMMM... NOT HERE, IT'S TOO SUNNY.

NOT HERE EITHER. THOSE BOYS WILL HURT MY TUR-TUR. WHERE DO I PARK YOU?

BIKER BOY

HE FINALLY PARKED HIS TUR-TUR JUST NEXT TO THE GUTTER.

NOBODY WILL COME ANYWHERE NEAR YOU, MY DEAR.

CRAZY?

BIKER BOY

AND SHAMBU MADE HIS WAY TO THE FAIR, HAPPY AND AT PEACE.

BUT CAN THERE BE PEACE AND NO ANIMAL IN SIGHT WHEN SHAMBU IS AROUND? NO WAY!

& TEA

% DIS

GARMENTS

SHAMBU, LOOK AT THAT ELEPHANT, ISN'T HE BEAUTIFUL?!

ULP! YES, YES.

HEY, YOU BIG FAT FELLOW!

WOULD YOU LIKE A NICE PAT?

OR A NICE WHACK!

STOP BOTHERING BUNTY, I SAY.

THWACK

BUNTY?

HA HA! BUNTY THE ELEPHANT!

SUCH A FUNNY NAME!

MY NAME IS FUNNY, EH?

SOMEBODY HAS TO DISCIPLINE THESE BRATS.

BUNTY REACHED UP TO THE MAHOUT...

HEY, BUNTY, STOP!

FREE TRIP TO

SORRY, BOSS. YOU'LL HAVE TO STEP DOWN FOR A WHILE.

...AND PUT HIM DOWN.

HE THEN REACHED DOWN TO THE BOYS...

YEOW! HELP!

WHAT IS HE DOING?!

JUST TAKING YOU FOR A LITTLE RIDE, BOYS.

...HOISTED THEM BOTH ON HIS BACK...

...AND BEGAN RUNNING.

EEYYAAAAA!!!

RUN, THERE'S AN ELEPHANT ON THE LOOSE!

THERE ARE TWO SMALL BOYS SITTING ON THE ELEPHANT!

THE PEOPLE SPOTTED SHAMBU

STOP THE ELEPHANT, MR SHAMBU, SAVE THE BOYS!

HE'S GETTING CLOSER TO THE GUTTER. HE'LL CRUSH MY TUR-TUR.

SHAMBU LEAPT FORWARD WITH A BLOOD-CURDLING

TUR-TUR! DON'T TOUCH MY TUR-TUR!

TUR-TUR? WHAT'S THAT?

MUST BE HIS WAR CRY.

SHAMBU GOT TO HIS BELOVED TUR-TUR BEFORE BUNTY COULD.

DON'T WORRY, TUR-TUR, I'M HERE NOW.

OOPS, MY LEG IS SLIPPING!

AS BUNTY'S LEG SLIPPED —

AAH, I AM FALLING!

YEOW!

S P L A T

YECH!

WHAT A STINK!

THAT'S WHAT YOU DESERVE.

LATER WHEN BUNTY HAD CALMED DOWN AND WAS TAKEN AWAY —

YOU MUST NEVER TEASE AN ANIMAL OR HIT IT, BOYS.

SOB! WE WON'T.

EVER AGAIN!

THAT WAS CLEVER OF YOU, MR SHAMBU TO DIVERT THE ELEPHANT TO THE GUTTER.

I ESPECIALLY LIKED YOUR WAR CRY, TUR-TUR!

ER...HEH HEH!

EVERYONE WAS TOO TERRIFIED TO DO ANYTHING. WELL, NOT EXACTLY 'EVERYONE'.

OUR WORLD LIES SHATTERED. WE MUST DO SOMETHING.

IT WAS PINKLE, THE SQUARE-HEADED SEA SERPENT.

HE CALLED OUT TO GEE, THE MERMAID.

PSST ... GEE ... LISTEN!

SHUSH! HE WILL HEAR YOU!

NO, HE WON'T. HE IS BUSY LOOKING AT HIS OWN REFLECTION IN THE MIRROR. GEE, WE HAVE TO GET RID OF HIM.

GASP! QUIET! YOU WILL BE KILLED FOR SUCH TALK.

LISTEN, ONCE AN EARTHLING WITCH WHO VISITED US TOLD ME THAT WIKIDO IS SCARED OF A WITCH CALLED JANOO. WE NEED HER HELP.

EARTH ! THAT IS MILLIONS OF MILES AWAY. HOW WILL WE CONTACT HER?

HAVE YOU FORGOTTEN THE COMMUNICATIONS ORB?

NO, I HAVEN'T. BUT IT IS UNDER A SPELL THAT KEEPS IT LOCKED WHEN WIKIDO IS NEAR BY.

YES, I KNOW. AND HE LOCKS IT WHEN HE IS AWAY. AND ONLY THE KING AND QUEEN CAN USE IT. AND WE SUBJECTS HAVE THE POWER TO USE IT ONLY FOR FIVE SECONDS AT MIDNIGHT ... I KNOW ALL THAT ...

... BUT I HAVE A PLAN, LISTEN ... BZZ ... BZZ... BZZ

TEE HEE !

AT MIDNIGHT TWO FIGURES CREPT TOWARDS WIKIDO'S CAVE ON THE SURFACE OF THE WATER.

THEN, AS PLANNED, GEE SHRIEKED.

JANOO IS HERE! HURRAH! JANOO! JANOO IS HERE!

WHA-A-A

WHERE ... WHERE ... WH...E ...R...E?

WIKIDO RAN STRAIGHT OUT INTO THE WATER.

SPLASH

AAAH!

PINKLE RUSHED IN TO THE UNLOCKED ORB.

JANOO ... HELP FLOATATE! HELP FLOATATE!

FIVE SECONDS WERE UP.

BLIP

I HAD BETTER VANISH.

JUST IN TIME TOO.

WAS I DREAMING? I HEARD SOMEONE YELL JANOO'S NAME. WHAT A NIGHTMARE!

FAR AWAY ON PLANET EARTH –

WOOLY, WAKE UP! I'VE HAD SUCH A LOVELY WALK IN JADU FOREST.

ORGGGHH ... JANOO! LET ME SLEEP. YOUR CRYSTAL BALL WAS MAKING SUCH A NOISE ... CRACKLE, CRACKLE... JABBER ... JABBER.

THERE IS A VERY WEAK SIGNAL. DID YOU HEAR ANYTHING?

UM ... UM ..., YES, SOMETHING LIKE 'HELP' 'FLOAT' AND THEN CRACKLE, AND THEN 'HATE' OR WAS IT 'HELP'?

JANOO THEN CALLED THE COMMUNICATOR REPAIR CENTRE.

NO, MA'AM, WE HAVE NOT RECEIVED ANY COMPLAINTS FROM FLOATATE.

THAT IS STRANGE.

JANOO, I DID HEAR, 'FLOAT' AND 'HATE'. IT COULD BE FLOATATE.

YOU ARE SMART, WOOLY. COME, LET'S CHECK.

THEY ZOOMED THROUGH GALAXIES, SHOT PAST BLACK HOLES AND SOON THEY WERE AT PLANET FLOATATE.

I'LL DISGUISE US AND WE'LL JOIN THAT PROCESSION. IT IS WIKIDO TROUBLE AS USUAL.

WIKIDO THE GREATEST

WIKIDO THE GREATEST

JANOO TURNED HERSELF INTO A SEA HORSE AND WOOLY WOO INTO A SEA SPONGE.

WIKIDO THE GREATEST

JANOO WITCH WILL COME

JANOO WITCH WILL COME

SOMEONE IS SAYING MY NAME. I THINK IT IS THE SERPENT THERE.

JANOO WITCH WILL COME.

DON'T TURN AROUND BUT I AM JANOO RIGHT BEHIND YOU ...

... MY FRIEND, WOOLY WOO, IS DISGUISED AS A SEA SPONGE WITH EYES.

OOOOH ! I AM PINKLE AND THIS IS GEE.

HERE'S MY PLAN ... BZZ ... BZZ.

AS PINKLE MOVED UP NEAR WIKIDO —

DOWN WITH WIKIDO! I AM MAKING US INVISIBLE.

GASP!

AAARGH! HOW DARE YOU! I'LL ZAP YOU WITH A HORRIBLE HEX TILL....

NO, YOU WON'T.

OW!

THUD

WHAM

WHOOSH

OW!

YAARGH!

AND HERE'S YOUR FAVOURITE RED CHILLI SPELL*

NO-O-O-O-O. JANOOOOOOOOO!

HURRAY! THE TYRANT HAS BEEN CONQUERED.

LATER AS THE MER KING AND MER QUEEN THANKED THE TWOSOME—

PINKLE AND GEE ARE THE HEROES. THEY DECIDED TO FIGHT WRONG WITHOUT CARING ABOUT THEMSELVES. THEY ARE BRAVE!

HURRAY FOR PINKLE AND GEE!

* THE RED CHILLI SPELL MADE WIKIDO DISSOLVE.

PUNYAKOTI

- A folktale from Karnataka.

Script:
Subba Rao
Illustrations:
K. Chandranath

HULIA THE TIGER WAS WEAK WITH HUNGER.

HE HAD NOT EATEN ANYTHING FOR DAYS.

IF I DON'T FIND SOME FOOD TODAY, I'LL DIE OF HUNGER.

JUST THEN—

TIN-TIN

WHAT'S THAT?

THE CATTLE RETURNING HOME AFTER GRAZING!

WHAT'S WRONG WITH ME? I COULDN'T CATCH A SILLY COW!

WHO DO I SEE COMING THIS WAY?

IT WAS A COW CALLED PUNYAKOTI.

I'D BETTER WALK FASTER. MY CHILD MUST BE WAITING FOR ME.

EH!

YES, I'VE BEEN WAITING FOR YOU.

HULIA, PLEASE LISTEN···

NO! I WON'T!

I AM GOING TO KILL YOU AND EAT YOU UP.

KILL ME! EAT ME! BUT NOT IMMEDIATELY.

MY CHILD IS WAITING FOR ME. I'LL GO HOME, FEED HIM AND COME BACK TO YOU.

WHAT!

HOHOHO!

DO YOU TAKE ME FOR A FOOL?

AS IF YOU'LL COME BACK, IF I LET YOU GO!

TINKLE DIGEST 300 DECEMBER 2016

BELIEVE ME, HULIA, I WILL. I GIVE YOU MY WORD WITH MOTHER EARTH AS A WITNESS.

ALL RIGHT, YOU MAY GO. BUT COME BACK SOON.

I WILL, HULIA, I WILL.

PUNYAKOTI RAN TO HER HOME AT THE FOOT OF THE HILL.

COME, MY CHILD!

DRINK, MY CHILD, DRINK AS MUCH MILK AS YOU CAN.

FOR THIS IS THE LAST TIME I WILL BE FEEDING YOU.

MOTHER!

YES, MY SON. I HAVE TO GO BACK TO HULIA. HE WILL BE WAITING FOR ME.

PUNYAKOTI TOLD HIM EVERYTHING ABOUT HER PROMISE TO HULIA.

BUT MOTHER, YOU DON'T HAVE TO GO BACK TO HULIA.

HE'S RIGHT. WE WILL AVOID THAT ROUTE, HULIA CAN'T DO A THING.

TINKLE DIGEST 300 DECEMBER 2016

MEANWHILE HULIA WAS GETTING IMPATIENT.

I SHOULDN'T HAVE LET HER GO.

SHE'LL NEVER COME...NO, THERE SHE IS!

SHE HAS KEPT HER PROMISE...EVEN THOUGH DEATH AWAITS HER HERE. WHAT A NOBLE CREATURE!

HULIA, MY BROTHER, COME! HERE I AM. EAT ME.

EAT YOU?

NEVER, MY NOBLE SISTER. NEVER.

GO BACK TO YOUR CHILD.

HULIA!

HULIA TURNED BACK AND LEFT.

AND PUNYAKOTI REJOINED HER CHILD.

SuperWeirdos: Thwacks!

Writer
Rajani Thindiath

Art
Abhijeet Kini

Letterer
Prasad Sawant

THE VILLAGE IS NOT SO BAD. IT HAS ITS SHARE OF INTERESTING CHARACTERS... EVEN SUPERHEROES... THOUGH THEY ARE SLIGHTLY WEIRD. IMAGINE, JUMPING AND CAUSING TREMORS ON EARTH!

BUT I'VE STILL NOT FIGURED OUT **MY** SUPERPOWER. IT EXISTS. IF ADA CAN HAVE ONE, EVEN THOUGH IT'S WEIRD...

...I CAN HAVE ONE TOO!

AISHA, COME ON, WE'RE OFF TO THE FAIR.

ALL OF YOU, LISTEN CAREFULLY. YOU'D BETTER HAVE MY WEEK'S COLLECTIONS READY WHEN I COME AROUND.

THE WRETCH...

...IF IT WEREN'T FOR THE MONEY WE'RE FORCED TO PAY HIM AND HIS GOONS, WE'D SEE SOME DECENT PROFITS.

SPARE ME THIS TIME, SHERA. I'VE NOT MADE A SINGLE SALE.

AND YOU THINK THAT IS MY PROBLEM BECAUSE...?

HEY, YOU!

YOU'VE LOST IT!

YOU CALLING ME, BOY? MISPLACED YOUR RESPECT, EH? DON'T WORRY, SHERA WILL TEACH YOU.

THE BOY'S MAD TO DRAW SHERA'S ATTENTION. HE'S HAD IT NOW!

(SNIGGER!)